The Monsoon Makers

Written by Susan Brocker
Illustrated by Marie Low

Cambodia

Kiri lives in Phnom Penh, the beautiful capital city of Cambodia. Kiri's grandparents come from Angkor, where the ancient temple ruins lie. When Kiri visits his grandparents, he likes to wander around the stone ruins. He feels as though he is stepping back in time.

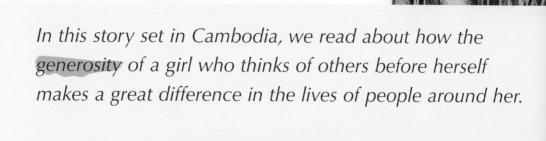

*In this story set in Cambodia, we read about how the
generosity of a girl who thinks of others before herself
makes a great difference in the lives of people around her.*

generosity giving freely to others

The delicate, raven-haired girl danced gracefully across the dry,
dusty ground. She swayed her body gently and twisted and
turned her slim hands and tapering fingers. Each movement
had a meaning, and together the movements told a story as old
as time.

Joruni watched as Kesor practiced her dance. She was supposed to be painting a bamboo screen for the stage, but she couldn't take her eyes off the dancers. Their school was putting on a dance-show retelling of an ancient legend about the creation of thunder and lightning. The legend has been danced in Cambodia for centuries to call forth the yearly monsoon rains that bring life to the dry land.

Joruni had prayed to the gods that she would be picked to dance, but her teacher had just smiled and said that she needed Joruni's help to build the set. Joruni looked down at her strong working hands and wished that they were fine and elegant like Kesor's. Kesor had the star role as the goddess, Moni Mekhala, and Samay had been chosen to dance opposite Kesor as the giant, Ream Eyso. Samay always teased Joruni, but she had to admit that he was a good dancer.

monsoon a season during which the winds bring heavy rainfall

In the legend, the goddess and giant were trying to impress a wise and powerful hermit who lived deep in the jungle. The hermit owned a glittering magic ball that he wanted to give to one of the dancers, but he could not decide who was more worthy. He, therefore, decided to put them both to a test. He told them to go out and collect the morning dew. Whoever collected the most dew would win the magic ball.

As Kesor and Samay rehearsed the dance, their teacher watched with a critical eye. At one point, she took Kesor's hand and gently bent it backward from the wrist to exercise the muscles. A dancer's hands and fingers needed to be supple and strong in order to make the smooth, wavelike movements needed in Cambodian classical dance.

Samay saw Joruni watching them and called over to her, "The paint is meant to go on the screen, not on your face!" He laughed. Joruni looked down at her hands. They were covered with green paint. She touched her face and realized that it must be covered with paint, too. She quickly picked up the brush and tried to concentrate on what she was doing until school was finally over for the day.

Joruni scampered home across the dusty paddy fields. She leaped over the dry irrigation ditches that divided the fields into neat patchwork squares. At this time of the year, the ditches were usually overflowing with water, and the paddy fields were a mosaic of green rice shoots. But the monsoon rains were late. The sun beat down fiercely from a cloudless sky, and even the banks of the mighty Mekong River were dry. The paddy fields lay bare and lifeless.

paddy a small plot of usually wet rice

Joruni joined her family as they worked on their small plot of land. Her father walked behind a water buffalo that pulled a wooden plow across the hard ground. Her mother and brothers followed, picking up stones turned up by the plow. It was hard work under the scorching sun. Joruni wrapped her krama, a long cotton scarf, around her head and neck to protect herself. She longed for the cool of the evening, when she could slip away on her own.

Once their chores were done, Joruni's brothers dashed off to play soccer with the other village children. It was Joruni's chance to escape. She tucked her sampot up around her waist and ran to the jungle on the outskirts of the village. Sunlight filtered through the branches of the towering trees. Everything was green and fresh after the dryness and heat of the fields. She followed a narrow track through the thick undergrowth until she came to her secret place.

sampot a skirt-like lower garment made of cotton or silk

The ruins of the ancient temple lay smothered by the jungle. Huge tree roots coiled around the broken pillars and crumbling walls. Two stone lions guarded what was once the doorway to the inner shrine. Joruni walked between them and laid her usual gifts of incense and flowers on the stone floor. The far wall of the temple stood supported by the spreading roots of a gigantic tree. Fantastic figures were carved into its sandstone blocks.

Joruni had traced the figures with the tips of her fingers time and again. They told stories of battles between good and evil. Warriors riding elephants fought off terrible creatures, men with animal faces marched against one-eyed giants, and serpents raised their hooded heads, ready to strike. Joruni's favorite figures were the rows of graceful apsara, heavenly creatures shown dancing for the gods. They seemed to glide across the wall, their elegant hands and fingers pointing at strange and wonderful angles. They wore high crowns on their heads and mysterious smiles upon their faces.

Joruni had studied the apsara and knew each and every one of their moves and gestures. She had seen her teacher showing some of the same moves to Kesor and Samay. In the privacy of the jungle, with only the birds to see her, Joruni also danced. She practiced the elegant hand movements and the graceful twists and turns. Her only music was birdsong and the chirping of cicadas. For one hour each day, she, too, was a beautiful and graceful apsara dancing in the heavens.

The following morning at school, Joruni watched from the shadows again as Kesor and Samay rehearsed scenes from the legend. Some of her classmates were dancing as gods and goddesses, and they also practiced. The dust swirled around their feet as they moved across the dry ground. Joruni had nearly finished painting the bamboo screen that was to form the backdrop of the outdoor stage. Other children were busy hand-sewing fancy costumes or painting colorful masks.

Their teacher talked them through the legend as she taught the dance moves to Kesor and Samay. The wise old hermit had just challenged the goddess, Moni Mekhala, and the giant, Ream Eyso, to collect the morning dew in order to win the magic ball. The giant thought it would be an easy task. He woke at dawn and gathered up leaves covered with droplets of dew. He squeezed them, one by one, into a glass and rushed back to the hermit with his prize.

But the goddess was far more clever. The night before, she had laid her handkerchief out upon the ground and then left it there overnight. In the morning, she picked up the soaking wet handkerchief and, with one squeeze, filled her whole glass with dew. The hermit awarded her the glittering magic ball. As a consolation prize, he gave the giant a magic ax. The giant was terribly jealous and flew into a rage.

Samay danced the role of the giant with great feeling. Joruni could see the anger in his quick movements and flashing eyes. But Kesor, dancing as the princess, seemed upset. When she bent to pick up the imaginary handkerchief, she nearly tripped. Joruni noticed that her usually graceful movements were clumsy and awkward. Suddenly, Kesor stopped dancing altogether and cried out, "I can't do this anymore!"

The class was stunned. Kesor broke down in tears and told the teacher that her parents needed her at home. She could no longer come to school or attend dance rehearsals. Their family was desperate because of the drought. If she did not help out in the fields, they would starve.

Joruni knew that Kesor's family was very poor. While nobody in the village was well off, most grew at least enough rice to feed their families. But Kesor's parents struggled to get by from season to season. Their small plot of land was stony and poor, and the irrigation ditches that once fed water to the fields were crumbling and blocked. There were no strong hands to repair the canals, because Kesor's brothers had left long ago to try to find work in the city. That left only Kesor, her elderly parents, and her grandmother to work the fields.

irrigate   to bring water to a place by way of ditches, canals, or pipes

Before Joruni knew what she was saying, she found herself calling out, "I can work in Kesor's place! I am much stronger than Kesor; the dance cannot go ahead without her." Kesor's face lit up. Joruni tried not to think of the hours of work ahead of her. At least the dance would be performed.

When Joruni told her parents about her offer to help Kesor's family, they were very proud. Joruni's father said he would take his buffalo over in the evenings, and they would work together to clear the ditches. In the meantime, Joruni would help Kesor's parents carry water to the newly transplanted rice seedlings before they withered and died.

Early the next morning, Joruni headed off to the fields. She walked past the village huts built on stilts to protect them from flooding in the rainy season. Chickens scratched in the dust beneath the huts, and Joruni wondered if the rains would ever come. She stopped at the small temple in the center of the village to give an offering of rice to the orange-robed monks and to ask for strength from the Buddha.

Buddha a figure representing the holy teacher Gautama Buddha

Kesor's parents were already at work when she arrived at their small plot far from the village. Kesor's grandmother was working alongside them, too. Joruni thought she must be at least in her eighties. Her face and hands were wrinkled and pitted from old age and years of hard work, but when she smiled at Joruni, she looked like a young girl again. "Thank you, child," the old woman said warmly to Joruni. "We need your strong, young bones!"

Joruni hoisted across her shoulders a long pole with large wooden buckets hanging from each end. She followed the others as they picked their way across the stony fields. It was a long walk to the nearest source of water, a river that was little more than a creek without the lifeblood of the monsoon rains. They struggled down its dry banks and laid the buckets in the muddy bed. Water trickled in and finally filled them. Then they trudged back with their heavy loads.

They walked up and down the raised rows of seedlings in their paddy and poured out the buckets of water. The young rice plants soaked up the water like thirsty sponges. Then the group turned and trudged back to the river to collect more. As the sun climbed high in the sky, the burning heat became almost unbearable. Kesor's grandmother put down her buckets and took a seat in the shade of a huge banyan tree. "Come, sit with me, child," she beckoned to Joruni. "Even young bones need a rest!"

Joruni joined the old woman in the welcome coolness of the shade. They chatted easily, and Joruni told her how much she admired her granddaughter. "Kesor is such a graceful dancer. I wish I could dance like that."

"Ah, but you could," said Kesor's grandmother. "All it takes is practice, determination, and a love of dance." The old woman told Joruni that when she was young, she had been a royal dancer. At the age of eight, she had gone to live in the Royal Palace in Phnom Penh for training. She had practiced for five hours every day to learn the thousands of moves and positions of Cambodian classical dance. She explained how each gesture of the hands and fingers had a meaning.

determination a drive to succeed

"Would you show me some of the moves?" Joruni asked. Kesor's grandmother laughed and said that her hands were no longer flexible enough. Instead, she took Joruni's hand and gently pushed back her fingers. "If you hold your hand and fingers like that, it represents a flower."

Over the next few weeks, Kesor's grandmother showed Joruni other hand movements in between the hard work. Then, no matter how tired she felt, Joruni would escape into the jungle to practice dancing. Now the moves of the apsara she saw carved into the walls of the temple made sense to her. She could read them like a story. Kesor's grandmother told her that royal dancers had danced before the kings of Angkor over one thousand years ago. The apsara had danced to please the gods.

Joruni worked long hours in the fields with Kesor's family. Joruni's father came each afternoon with his water buffalo to help clear the ditches. When the rains finally arrived, the waterways would be needed to store and channel water to the paddy fields. Joruni walked behind one of the buffalo as it dragged a harrow through the ditches. She held the long traces hitched to a wooden yoke around the buffalo's huge neck. She clucked quietly to the slow-moving animal, urging him on.

One hot afternoon, Joruni had a visitor. She and Kesor's grandmother were resting in the shade when she heard a sassy voice call out, "So this is what you call hard work!" Samay strolled up and tossed a pineapple to Joruni. "It's freshly picked," he said. "I thought you might enjoy it on such a hot day." He told Joruni that the dance rehearsals at school were going well, though the set still needed a lot of work. Kesor's emerald-green silk costume was nearly finished, and so was the fierce-looking giant's mask that he would wear.

To Joruni's surprise, Samay stayed on and helped them carry bucketloads of water back and forth from the river. He was strong and fast, and even his lighthearted teasing made the task easier. But they all knew that the amount of water was barely enough to keep the young rice seedlings alive. Without the monsoon rains, the seedlings would not grow and ripen. Everybody in the village was worried now. Even the village well was running dry.

harrow a tool used in farming to break up and smooth soil

From then on, Samay was a regular helper. As soon as school and dance rehearsals were finished, he would turn up with a smile and a joke. Kesor, too, helped when she could, and some of the other village children lent a hand in between school and their own chores at home.

Meanwhile, the whole village looked forward to the dance performance. Traditionally, the dance was performed to entertain the gods and ask them to send the monsoon rains. It was believed that if the gods and spirits were pleased with the dance, they would allow the rains to fall. Nobody in the village could remember a time when rain was more needed. After work, many of the adults gathered at the school to help finish building the set as well as the raised wooden stage on which the dance play would be performed outside the schoolhouse.

Joruni couldn't wait to see the dance. She knew all the moves now, and she still practiced every evening in front of the temple ruins. It didn't matter to her that only the birds would ever see her perform. Even though her muscles ached from the day's work, she felt wonderfully happy as she danced. The scent of burning incense and lotus blossom drifted through the cool evening air, and horseshoe bats swirled and dived among the ruins.

Two days before the dance performance was scheduled to be staged, Joruni visited the temple ruins as usual. It had been another hot, cloudless day with no sign of the monsoon rains. Joruni lit an incense stick at the feet of one of the carved apsara dancers. Then she unwrapped the krama scarf from her head and let her long, dark hair fall freely down her back. She slipped off her sandals and began to dance.

Joruni practiced for half an hour before she sensed that she was being watched. She saw a movement out of the corner of her eye and turned to find Samay leaning against one of the stone lions that guarded the temple. "How long have you been there?" she asked. She could feel her face reddening.

"Long enough to see that you're a good dancer. I wondered where you were sneaking off to every evening," Samay said.

Joruni picked up her shoes and her krama. "Please don't tell anyone. They would only laugh."

"There's nothing to laugh at," Samay said. "You're great!"

Joruni slipped past him without saying a word and ran home.

The next afternoon, Samay and Kesor went together to the
field where Joruni was working. Samay had told Kesor about
her skillful dancing, and she asked if Joruni would show her.
Joruni shook her head. "No, I'm not good at all. I just enjoy it."

Kesor's grandmother was listening. "Why don't you let me be
the judge of that? Come, child, show us," she encouraged.

Reluctantly, under the shade of the banyan tree where
Kesor's grandmother had taught her so many moves, Joruni
danced barefoot in the dust. The old lady watched, her eyes
glistening. She said to Joruni, "You dance as gracefully as the
apsara carved on the ancient temple walls."

reluctant   to be unwilling or hesitant to do something

Kesor asked Joruni if she would dance alongside her in the performance. "You could play the part of an apsara dancing in the heavens!"

"But I have no costume, and the dance is tomorrow night," said Joruni with resignation.

"Ah, but I do!" Kesor's grandmother said. "I played the part of the apsara in my youth. It was the highest honor for a dancer. I have kept the costume all these years."

That evening, Joruni visited Kesor's grandmother. After supper, she strolled slowly along the dusty village and climbed the ladder to Kesor's family hut. The old woman slept in a covered verandah built on the front of the wooden hut. Its roof was made from palm leaves, and it was furnished with a sleeping mat and a large bamboo chest.

From the bamboo chest, Kesor's grandmother pulled out a glittering tunic made of red and gold silk and a tall, golden crown. Joruni had never seen anything more splendid. "Will it fit me?" she asked. "I am not tiny like Kesor."

"When I was your age, I was tall and strong, too," Kesor's grandmother said. "The costume will be perfect for you." She was right. Joruni slipped the beautiful red and gold tunic over her head, and it fit like a glove. She felt as though she were dancing in the heavens already.

resignation *giving up all hope*

On the night of the performance, the sky was inky black, and the air was hot and sticky. All the performers were nervous and excited as they waited backstage. This was the big night. Joruni touched the rich fabric of her costume nervously. Kesor had said she looked lovely, and even Samay had looked at her admiringly. Joruni thought they all looked dazzling in their glittering costumes and bright masks.

The villagers gathered at the small temple, and boys carrying bright lanterns led them to the outdoor stage. When they were all seated on mats on the ground, the boys walked up on stage and formed a circle of light. The musicians knelt at the front of the stage. The atmosphere was electric. Then Kesor and Samay danced into the circle of lanterns. The rich colors of their costumes and Samay's mask glittered and glowed in the firelight. The Legend of Moni Mekhala and Ream Eyso had begun.

29

The villagers followed the story eagerly. The hermit awarded the glittering magic ball to Moni Mekhala, and the giant flew into a jealous rage. He chased the princess into the heavens, where she danced with the gods and goddesses. At this moment, Joruni entered the stage as the beautiful apsara. She danced as she had never danced before. The villagers were entranced.

Suddenly the jealous giant hurled his magic ax at Moni Mekhala. The ax flew across the sky, making a thunderous roar. It barely missed her. She took up her glittering magic ball and flung it furiously at the giant. It lit up the heavens in a bolt of lightning.

The cymbals crashed out the thunder, and flaming torches flashed the lightning. Kesor, Samay, Joruni, and the other performers danced the eternal battle between thunder and lightning. The stage was alive with the storm. The villagers loved it. They cheered and applauded the dancers.

The gods and spirits must have enjoyed the dance, too, for as the villagers clapped, the sky above them opened up, and the rain began to fall. In the paddy fields, the rice seedlings lifted up their wilted heads and drank thirstily. The monsoon rains had finally arrived.

Discussion Starters

1 When Joruni volunteered to take Kesor's place in the fields, she knew that she would miss out on the fun of the dance show and would instead have to do a great deal of hard work. What kind of person do you think Joruni was to do this?

2 If you were Kesor, how would you feel about Joruni? How would you show your gratitude?

In the end, Joruni was rewarded for her generosity. Do you think most people would have offered to help out in the way that Joruni did?